Night Music

by Pat Cummings

Illustrated by Anthony Accardo

Macmillan/McGraw–Hill

Columbus, Ohio

Something's bumping
by the bed,
someone's jumping
overhead.

2

Whispers whispering
by the door,
something's sliding
'cross the floor.

Kali sits straight up
in bed,
squints her eyes,
and turns her head.

"Mom!" she calls,
and looks around.
"In the dark,
I heard a sound."

4

"Hush now, Kali,
not a peep!
By now you should be
fast asleep!"

"But Mom, there's some-
thing dark and furry..."
"Sleep now," Mom says,
"don't you worry."

"I'll leave a light on
in the hall,
and if you need me,
give a call."

Mom tucks Kali in
so tight.
One hug, one kiss,
and then good night.

This new house makes
sounds at night.
Things seem to happen
out of sight.

No matter how hard
Kali tries,
she's too afraid
to close her eyes.

"Mom!" she calls,
and Mom appears.
Kali tells her
all she hears.

"Granny says,
the sounds you hear
are music of a kind,
my dear."

"Yes, Granny says that all the trees *do* hum and whistle in the breeze."

Granny's old sweater hung on her chair. When Granny left, she'd left it there.

11

Mom tiptoes in,
picks up the sweater.
"Wrap this around,
you'll feel better."

"I'll think of all the sounds
as music in the night."
Then Kali rubs her eyes,
and pulls the sweater tight.

13

She heard a whistle
like a flute,
a thump, a crack,
and then a hoot.

She heard a squeak,
a bump, a song,
but Kali simply
hummed along.